MW00760457

WELCOME TO ROARSVILLE

Based on the series created by Niamh Sharkey
Written by Sheila Sweeny Higginson
Illustrated by Premise Entertainment

DISNEY PRESS

Los Angeles • New York

WELCOME TO MY TOWN!

I'm Henry Hugglemonster, and this is my town, Roarsville.
Roarsville is the most monsterrific place in the whole wide world!

Cobby

Megabouncer
Boots

tree

Roarsville

Momma

watering
can

Ivo

pumpkins

rake

Daddo

PUMPKIN
PATCH

roof

MY HOUSE

weather
vane

cloud

window

SUMMER'S
STAGE

Summer

tutu

door

Beckett

Henry
(that's me)

MY HUGGLEHOUSE

MY ROOM

mirror

books

pillow

blanket

bed

toys

desk

OUR KITCHEN

MUSIC SHED

gong

drum

fluegeltar

bass

window

monstercakes

cupboard

breadbox

sink

stove

table

high chair

refrigerator

Daddo's in the kitchen making monstercakes.

My family travels around in monsterstyle.
Check out our Hugglebike.
We all work together to keep it rolling.

That's what I call teamwork!

cloud

monsterbirds

light

cap

whistle

horn

Officer Higgins

belt

handlebars

seat

gear

wheel

pedal

road

monsterflowers

NEIGHBORS AND FRIENDS

There are all kinds of monsters in Roarsville.
My friend Estelle is an Enormomonster.
Everything in her house is HUGE!

Denzel is a Dugglemonster.
He's roarsome at digging holes and tunnels.

MONSTERSCHOOL

Roarsville has Furrymonsters and Glowingmonsters. There are Wavemonsters, Cloudmonsters, and Spikymonsters, too!

clock

CLASSROOM

ROARING 101

blackboard

teacher

ROARSOME

pencils

me

students

desk

We all go to Monsterschool together.
We learn the things that will make us monsterrific.

doors

sharpener

BE SHARP bulletin board

Cobby

Summer

MONSTER SAFETY

Denzel

THE PARK

My friends and I love to play in Roarsville Park.
Huggleball is the most roarsome game ever!

THE ROARSVILLE
ROARERS TEAM

Gertie

Denzel

me

Mrs. Dugglemonster

goal

Grando

Mr. Dugglemonster

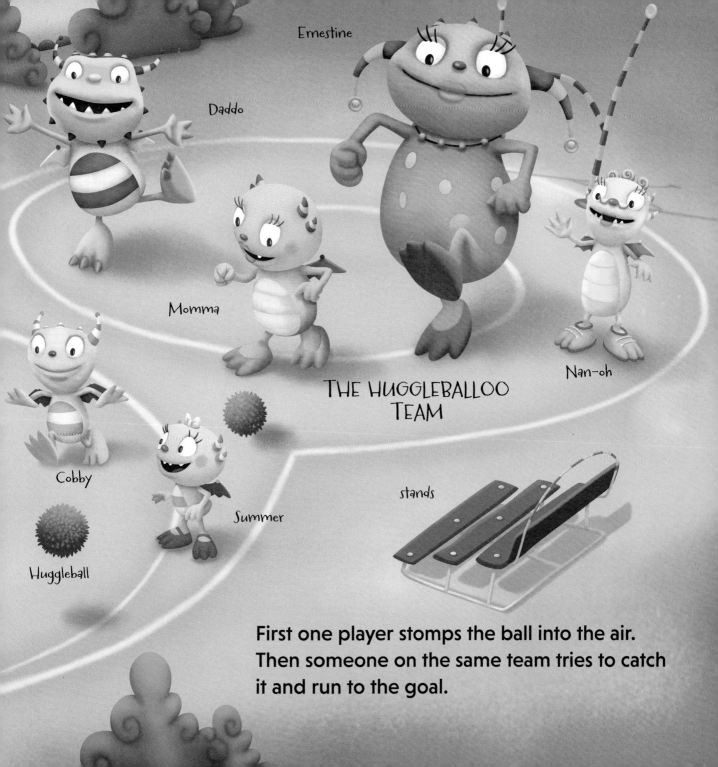

Ernestine

Daddo

Momma

THE HUGGLEBALLOO
TEAM

Nan-oh

Cobby

Summer

stands

Huggleball

First one player stomps the ball into the air.
Then someone on the same team tries to catch
it and run to the goal.

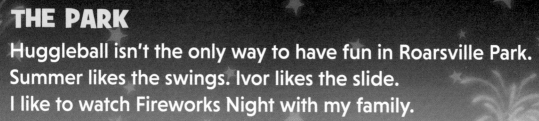

THE PARK

Huggleball isn't the only way to have fun in Roarsville Park.
Summer likes the swings. Ivor likes the slide.
I like to watch Fireworks Night with my family.

swing

slide

cup

cookies

apple

basket

sandwich

picnic table

stars

fireworks

Hugglebike

flashlight

blanket

THE RESTAURANT

Signor Roartonio owns a restaurant
in the center of town.
He makes the most roarsome
spaghetti and monsterballs.

RESTAURANT

spaghetti

serving tray

monsterballs

bowl

knife

plate

table

cup

fork

spoon

chair

Signor
Roartonio

menu

THE BAKERY

Momma likes to stop by the bakery for dessert.
Mr. Dugglemonster always has sweet treats for us.
Yummy!

THE SHOPS

My favorite comic book is *The Mighty Roarhammer*.
I head to Mr. Growlerstein's newsstand
whenever a new issue comes out.

MR. GROWLERSTEIN'S
NEWSSTAND

newspapers

The Mighty
Roarhammer

comic books

Matilde owns the Roarsville Art Shop. She can appreciate an artistic masterpiece.

Rainbow Falls

raft

log

paddles

rock

Daddo is the leader of my Monster Scout troop.
He takes us camping at Rainbow Falls.

It's fun to roast S'More Roars and listen to
Daddo tell stories about the Spooky River Monster.

tent

Hugglefish

pillow

sleeping bag

S'More Roars

campfire

MOUNT ROARSMORE

When it snows in Roarsville, we all grab our sleds and head to Mount Roarsmore.

Mount Roarsmore

snowflakes

footprints

tracks

hat

scarf

earmuffs

snow

sled

icicle

gloves

Ernestine
Enormomonster

snowmonster

coat

Eduardo
Enormomonster

Some monsters say there's a scary Snow-Grrr there,
but I know that's silly.
We're the only monsters around, and we're not scary at all!

So, what do you think of Roarsville?
Pretty roarsome, right?

Books based on your favorite Disney Junior shows!

These books and more are available wherever books and eBooks are sold.

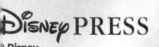
© Disney

WELCOME TO ROARSVILLE

Henry Hugglemonster lives in Roarsville, the best place ever! Roarsville is filled with all kinds of monsters and plenty of fun things to do. Stop by for a visit. You're welcome anytime!

DADDO
Daddo is Postmonster General of Roarsville, half of the roarsome duo t[...] leads the Hugglemonster household and the best juggler in town!

MOMMA
The only thing Momma loves more th[...] her music is her family. She's a talente[...] musician who gives lessons at home [...] she can stay close to her little monste[...]

HENRY
Henry is a friendly little monster who knows that Hugglemonsters always f[...] a way. He loves trying new things, ev[...] when they don't work out exactly as planned.

SUMMER
Summer is Henry's big sister. She sing[...] dances, and puts on spectacular show[...] for her friends and family.

COBBY
If you need a master inventor, Cobby [...] the Hugglemonster to call. The oldes[...] of the Hugglemonster siblings, Cobb[...] loves building things to solve proble[...]

IVOR
Ivor is the baby of the family. He's curious about everything and everyo[...]

BECKETT
The family monsterpet loves to spend quality time with all the Hugglemonsters.

$4.99 US/$5.50 CAN
ISBN 978-148470264-2

Disney PRESS

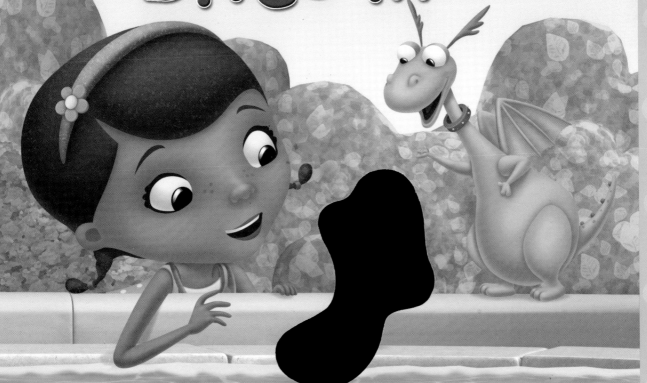

The Mermaid Dives In

Meet the Gang

Doc McStuffins

Doc McStuffins is a doctor for stuffed animals and toys. She has a magic stethoscope that can bring her toys to life! Doc loves helping her friends when they aren't feeling their best. She makes sure to write down each diagnosis in her Big Book of Boo-Boos.

Lambie

Lambie is Doc's stuffed lamb who just loves to cuddle! She doesn't like to get dirty and always tries to look her best.

Stuffy

Stuffy is a silly but brave stuffed dragon. His greatest wish is to be a real dragon. Whether Stuffy is trying to fly or helping out, he's always good for a laugh.

Hallie

Hallie is Doc's lovable hippo receptionist. She keeps things running smoothly. Hallie is always ready to give Doc a helping hand, but that doesn't mean she doesn't know how to have fun!

Chilly

Chilly is a nervous stuffed snowman. He's constantly worried that he will melt. But Doc always reminds him that he's not a real snowman.

ISBN 978-1423171132-4

EAN

Disney PRESS

First Edition
ISBN 978-1-4231-7132-4

G658-7729-4-13249

Manufactured in the USA
For more Disney Press fun, visit www.disneybooks.com